POKÉMON DP Galactic Battles

MEET CYNDAQUIL

Adapted by Simcha Whitehill from the episode "An Egg Scramble"

No part of this work may be reproduced in whole or in part, or stored in a retrieval system, or transmitted in any form or by any means, electronic, mechanical, photocopying, recording, or otherwise, without written permission of the publisher. For information regarding permission, write to Scholastic Inc., Attention: Permissions Department, 557 Broadway, New York, NY 10012.

ISBN 978-0-545-34172-1

12 11 10 9 8 7 6 5 4 3 2 1   10 11 12 13 14 15/0

Designed by Cheung Tai
Printed in the U.S.A.   40
This edition, first printing, January 2011

SCHOLASTIC INC.

New York   Toronto   London   Auckland
Sydney   Mexico City   New Delhi   Hong Kong

Ash, Dawn, and Brock were on their way to Lilypad Town for a big Pokémon Contest.

"*Marill, Mar!*" they heard a Pokémon cry.

"*Piplup, Pip!*" said Dawn's Piplup, pointing. A little Marill was stuck in between two buildings.

Piplup and Pikachu ran over to help the Aqua Mouse Pokémon. Together, they grabbed Marill and pulled.

"*Pikaaaaaaaa!*" Pikachu yelped.

Pop! Marill came free.

Just then, a girl ran up to the little group.

"Does this Marill belong to you?" Dawn asked her.

"It sure does! Lyra's the name," she said. "Hi!"

Lyra told them she was traveling through town, too. She worked for a festival that featured special food, sights, and Pokémon from the Johto region.

"That reminds me, I've got something cool to show you," Lyra said.

Lyra led Ash, Dawn, Brock, Piplup, and Pikachu to the festival grounds.

"This is the Johto Festival," she explained.

"Wow, Johto . . . great memories!" said Ash, looking around.

Lyra introduced the kids to her friend Khoury and his dad.

"Hey, a Totodile!" Dawn exclaimed. She'd never seen one before.

Khoury's Totodile didn't want to say hello. This Totodile was a picky eater. It didn't like its Pokémon food.

"I think it may be a tad sweet," Brock said.

Brock mixed some Chesto
Berries into the Pokémon food.
He served it to Totodile. The little
Water-type gobbled it all up!
   "Thank you so much! That's
great," Khoury cheered.

Totodile leaped up onto Khoury's shoulder. "*Totodile, Toto!*"

"I think it's trying to let you know the show's going to start," Khoury told Lyra.

"Whoa! I almost forgot," said Lyra. "It's an exhibition of all the Johto Pokémon!" she told Ash and his friends. "Why don't you guys check it out?"

Lyra was the star of the show. She stepped up on the stage with a wide smile.

"Hello, people of Sinnoh!" Lyra shouted. "Are you feeling GREAT?"

In the crowd, Ash, Dawn, Brock, Pikachu, and Piplup clapped.

Lyra brought out Chikorita.
"In Johto, new Trainers have
a choice between Chikorita,
Cyndaquil, and Totodile for their
first Pokémon," she explained.
"*Chiko!*" cried Chikorita.
It was excited to see so many
people at the fair.

Lyra challenged Dawn and
Piplup to battle for a special prize.
"All right, Piplup, let's go!"
Dawn said.
"*Piplup!*" Piplup nodded.

Chikorita used Razor Leaf. *Swish!*
Piplup blasted it with BubbleBeam.
Bam!
Chikorita blocked it with Light
Screen. *Pow!*

"Piplup, use Peck to break through!" Dawn shouted.

"*Piplup!*" Piplup broke through Chikorita's Light Screen. It won the match!

"Congratulations!" Lyra said.

Lyra handed Dawn her prize, a mystery Pokémon Egg.

"Awesome!" Dawn said. "Thank you, Lyra!"

"The question now is what kind of Pokémon is inside that Egg!" said Lyra. "You'll have to wait and see."

But suddenly....

"Team Rocket!" Ash yelled. The Pokémon thieves' hot-air balloon was floating above the festival.

"Check out that Pokémon Egg!" cried Meowth, snatching the Egg.

"Have a nice day!" cried Jessie, James, and Meowth as they flew off.

Then Team Rocket hit a tree.
It poked a hole in their balloon.
   "*Aaahhhhhhh!*" they screamed
as the balloon shot across the sky.
   Team Rocket crashed somewhere
in the woods.

"Let's get that Egg back!" Ash said.

"Hey, I want to come, too!" said Lyra. "Wait!"

"Uh . . . good luck," Khoury said.

"You're coming with me and that's that!" Lyra told him.

After they landed, Team Rocket had lunch in the woods. A Teddiursa approached them and tried to take a bite of their food.

"Stop! That's my food!" cried Jessie, shooing Teddiursa away.

Then an angry Ursaring burst in on their picnic. *"Urrrrrr!"* it yelled.

"We made Junior cry, and now we're going to fry!" Meowth cried.

Ursaring chased after Team Rocket, aiming Hyper Beam at them. Jessie was so scared, she dropped the Pokémon Egg. James and Meowth made a quick turn to save it. Ursaring kept running after Jessie.

Meanwhile, Ash and his friends were walking through the woods, looking for Team Rocket.

"Now, where'd they go?" Ash asked.

"Let's split up and look," said Brock.

"Staraptor! Fly around and look for Team Rocket!" Ash said, taking out a Poké Ball.

Staraptor flew through the sky searching for Team Rocket.

"*Starrraptor, Starrr!*" Staraptor said, pointing its wing.

Ash, Brock, and Khoury started running toward Staraptor. Soon they'd caught up with Team Rocket.

"No! It's a twerp bust!" cried
Meowth.

"Give me back my Egg right now!"
cried Dawn. She and Lyra had circled
around behind Team Rocket.

The Pokémon thieves were
surrounded!

"Carnivine, assistance!" James cried, calling on one of his favorite Pokémon.

"Carni–mmm!" said Carnivine, sinking its chompers into James's head.

"*OWWWW!*" cried James.

Totodile ran up and snatched the
Egg back from Team Rocket.
   "Way to go, Totodile!" Khoury said.
   But Team Rocket still wanted to
battle.

Pikachu hit Team Rocket with Thunderbolt. *Whap!*

Piplup fired off BubbleBeam. *Whoosh!*

Totodile and Marill both used Water Gun. *Splat!*

James, Meowth, and Carnivine blasted off!

"I guess that settles things!" Lyra cheered.

"The Egg's fine! What a relief!" Dawn said.

Back at the festival, Lyra and Khoury told Khoury's dad they wanted to go to Lilypad Town with their new pals. Lyra wanted to see her first Contest, and Khoury wanted Brock to teach him some new Pokémon tips.

"Sure! That'd be fine," Ash said.

All of a sudden, the Egg started
glowing. It was hatching!
It was a little Cyndaquil!

"Cyndaquil, it's nice to meet you!"
Dawn cried. "My name's Daw—"

"*Cyndaaaaa!*" said Cyndaquil. Its
back flamed up, scorching Dawn's
hair.

When it came to certain Pokémon,
Dawn had a history of bad hair days.

"That's hot!" Dawn said, coughing.
Everyone laughed. They couldn't
wait to continue their journey with
their new friends and Dawn's newest
Pokémon.

Flip over this book to read "The Runaway Pokemon"!